The Great Ringtail
Garbage Caper

Weekly Reader Books presents

The Great Ringtail Garbage Caper

BY TIMOTHY FOOTE

Illustrated by Normand Chartier

Houghton Mifflin Company Boston 1980

The author wishes to thank the real Nip Jordans and Tuck Taylors of the island, whose cheerfulness and efficiency should long since have driven raccoons to take matters into their own hands.

Library of Congress Cataloging in Publication Data

Foote, Timothy.
    The great ringtail garbage caper.

    SUMMARY: A group of desperate and daring raccoons
organize a bold hijacking scheme when their lush food
supply is threatened by a pair of efficient young
garbage collectors.
    [1. Raccoons – Fiction.   2. Refuse and refuse
disposal – Fiction]   I. Chartier, Normand, 1945-
II. Title.
PZ7.F7473Gr   [Fic]   79-21238
ISBN 0-395-28759-6

For ATF, *who listened and* JTF, *who could read aloud better than anybody in the world*

Contents

The Great Ringtail
Garbage Caper

1.

Nip and Tuck

The island was trimmed with white sand and lay in a blue sea. Each July and August it became a paradise of screaming gulls and sunburned children, sailboats and swordfishermen, cocktail parties and raccoons who lived off the fat leavings of the summer folk. So many off-islanders kept crowding over from the mainland, in fact, that the real islanders sometimes felt as if the whole island might sink. But year after year it floated serenely in place.

Up island, near a fishing village where the sea cuts a deep channel inland, everybody was used to the way the garbage got collected. Sloppily. Twice a week an old Chevy truck with a round tank bumped over pitted roads from house to house. Two surly young men would climb out, clank the cans around, and then drive off,

1

usually leaving trails of trash along the way. Sometimes they forgot to come at all. Then householders were set upon by raiding parties of raccoons, or had to wrestle their cans into a car and drive to the dump — a dreadful, smoky place presided over by bloody-beaked gulls in the daytime, and by raccoons at night. The garbage boys were supposed to burn and bury their load but they seldom took time to do it properly. That was all right with the gulls, and with the raccoons, who not only sorted through the garbage before it was picked up, but considered the dump a fine supermarket where mothers and little kids regularly stopped to pick up delicacies.

All this was before Nip Jordan and Tuck Taylor appeared. When they were hired for the garbage job, everybody figured they'd be just like garbage boys from ages past. But Nip and Tuck figured differently. Bound for Yale, and bristling with ambition, they felt that a garbage truck was as good a vehicle as any to put them on the road to success. Right off they gave the old truck a new name, *Esmeralda,* and a fresh coat of white enamel. On its rear end they painted a picture of a seagull trying to fly away with a loaded garbage can. On one side of the truck they blocked in the words: CLIMB IN PEACHES, HERE'S YOUR CAN. Then they printed: WASTE NOT, WANT NOT, and under that came the two boys' signatures, painted out in longhand.

They usually finished their run on the sixty Up Island

families just before dawn, when the weather was still cool. They tried hard not to clang the cans around in the dark, and they never left behind a trail of eggshells, orange peels, or goldy bits of margarine wrapping. At the dump they promptly burned or buried all the garbage before heading home to clean up. Soon, whenever Nip and Tuck came by to collect the regular fee, mothers and fathers were happily throwing in an extra five dollars out of sheer gratitude.

Everybody on the island was overjoyed except the raccoons. The first bad news came from whiny kits who scuttled off to one local garbage can or another for a morning snack, only to come back snivelling. "Mommy, Mommy," they would squeak, running home through the shadowy, secret trails that led under a green tent of grapevine and scrub oak, "there's no peanut butter." Or whatever there happened not to be. Then raccoon fathers, stopping off in the dusk on their way home for a few ripe olives or a slice of Camembert rind, began to reach their nests hungry — and very grumpy too. It was not long, in fact, before the garbage crisis, as it came to be known, grew very sharp indeed. So sharp that an emergency meeting of the Benevolent Protective Society of Raccoons was called at the BPSR Community Center in the basement hall of the white, pillared Methodist church.

"Friends and fellow ringtails," said the Oldest Raccoon, looking at the assembled coons over the top of a pair of pince-nez originally found for him at the dump by his nephew Ezra. "There *is* a crisis. The shortage is real. But keep calm, it's unlikely to last. 'Where man is, there shall garbage be also,' says the *Great Book of Raccoondom.* That has always been so. In the meantime we must all tighten our belts."

"Tighten our belts!" exclaimed a large mother raccoon who had jumped up way in the back near the door. "I have ten starving kits at home. They don't even *have* belts, poor hungry things." There was a general murmur of sympathy.

"There's no need to go hungry, ma'am," the Oldest Coon replied sternly. "Raccoons lived on the island long before men came. It is full of natural foods. They're all tasty and fairly easy to catch. In fact, for those parents and children who have forgotten what raccoons *used* to eat I've put together a list." He stopped, looked up into one corner of the room, and began reciting: "Frogs, toads, tadpoles, newts, salamanders, hermit crabs, crawfish, snails, grasshoppers, beach plums, and baby horseshoe crabs."

Groans rose from all the little raccoons as the list proceeded. And most of the raccoon families grumbled a good bit as they left the meeting. The Oldest Coon was famous for his wisdom, however. It was even believed that he had once been off the island, stowing away as a youth on the ferry S.S. *Pierce* and spending several years in Cambridge, Massachusetts, where he lived off food left over from faculty club luncheons at a famous university, thus picking up tidbits of learning. He was regarded as a bit of a back number because he kept telling everyone that sugar is bad for the teeth. But the other raccoons knew that he kept a sharp eye on what was happening in the strange world of men. He alone had the right to sit in the crotch of the scraggly cedar tree that grows beside Ezra Norton's glassed-in porch and provides a fine view of the Norton television set.

At first, most raccoon families tried to do exactly what the Oldest Coon had advised. It was easy for the mothers and fathers. Many of them had actually grown up eating tadpoles. But the scenes that went on between the parents and baby coons, and the sounds that rose from the raccoon kits at suppertime were truly dreadful. Raccoon mothers did their best. Some tried to dress up the natural food brought in dripping (and sometimes wriggling) from swamps and creeks. Supreme of Crawfish was one result. Snailtail Patty was another. A few mothers tried to transform the rough fare into a fair substitute for foods that had become part of the modern raccoon diet. Newtburgers in ketchup (most families still had some ketchup left over from easier times) was lovingly served. So were Prime Ribs of Salamander and a delicious dessert called Toad in the Hole. To no avail. From hollow tree and sandy burrow, the length and breadth of the island, a chorus of high, chittering complaint rose on the night air — mostly from young coons deprived for the first time in their lives of such things as Cocoa Puffs, Pringles, Bumble Bee tuna and Del Monte asparagus tips. Not to mention special treats like anchovy, marshmallow delight, and caviar.

"Beach plums, yecch! I want Smuckers!" howled Bobby B. Coon, age four years, of Lobsterville. "Newt-burgers for others," declared Debbie C. Coon, seven, of Herring Creek. "Ugh! Not grasshoppers *again*!" moaned Everett B. Coon, five, of Gull Island. "Mussels stink!" snarled Rodney Vandercoon, six, and was sent straight to bed. "I wish these old horseshoe crabs would just gallop away," sobbed Jessica R. Coon, eight. But of course they didn't.

2.

The Daring Dozen

Parents were in despair. And soon another complication set in. The supply of easily collected toads, tadpoles, frogs, newts, and grasshoppers began to run out. Because so many people now came to the island, there was much less room for wetlands where such things are found. And because raccoons had enjoyed such rich leavings for so long, there were a great many more coons on the island than ever before, too. A big, new emergency meeting was called.

This time every Up Island coon and coonlet clustered together in the church basement. They were buzzing and chittering with dismay when the Oldest Coon arrived to call the meeting to order.

"Friends and neighbors," he began. "I'm very sorry to report that our situation has not improved."

"Right on, Ol' Granddad," shouted a rude, rednecked coon in the front row. And soon everybody was shouting. "What'll we do?" "My Gregory simply won't touch crawfish!" "Herring Creek is fresh out of frogs!" In the back someone was holding up a sign that read: NATURAL FOODS, FAUGH! A second placard read: NO NEWTS IS GOOD NEWTS.

"Order, Order!" growled the Oldest Coon. He began pointing for attention, slamming a desk top with an old paintbrush as a gavel. "We'll never get anything done like this. We're here because the crisis has gotten worse."

"Hear! Hear!" everybody cried.

"And by the crisis," continued the Oldest Coon, "I don't mean all the whining I've heard from young coons too spoiled to eat." Here the Oldest Coon glared down upon a row of youngsters near the front. "Nor do I mean the trouble caused by fathers and mothers," here he shifted his disapproving glance to the entire company, "by fathers and mothers, I say, who have forgotten how to see that they are obeyed! Some of you have clean forgotten the first rules of raccoon parenthood:

RULE 1 ASK AS LITTLE AS POSSIBLE OF KITS
RULE 2 BUT DON'T TAKE NO FOR AN ANSWER

If your kit won't eat what's served, send him to bed without supper."

Groans from all the young raccoons at the meeting.

The Oldest Coon paused to look over the whole company. "No," he continued, "the real problem is still those dratted garbage boys. I thought they'd soon get tired of doing their job so well. But they haven't. And now we'll have to do something about them."

"Just let me at 'em," shouted a gruff voice from the back. "I'll gnaw their blasted tires flat!"

"Not me," growled another. "I'd wait in the dark by the dump and slash their ankles to the bone."

"Now you're talkin'," a third voice chimed in. "Only we gotta get organized. Teams of ankle-slashers at every garbage stop. That'll learn 'em."

A cheer rose from the crowd. Mingled cries of "Cut 'em! Slash 'em!" resounded through the hall. The Oldest Coon banged hard with his paintbrush.

"Order! Order!" he called again. When, at last, the meeting settled down once more he looked at his fellow raccoons and sadly shook his head.

"As long as I am head coon there will be no slashing. Or cutting. Or any foolishness such as that. Because it won't work."

Cries of "Why won't it?" and "Serve 'em right!" rang through the hall.

"In the whole history of raccoondom," replied the Oldest Coon, "no animal has ever fought man and won. Dogs, maybe, once in a while in desperation. Man never. Soon as you slash an ankle and man learns about

it, he will set his dogs on you. And put out poison bait. And you and your wives and kits will all be killed."

Cries of "What'll we do, then?" were heard.

"I'll tell you," answered the Oldest Coon. "First of all, the First Selectcoon has made a fine suggestion. From now on, instead of each family hunting just for itself, we'll have teams of hunters, working for everybody. One to work Herring Creek for frogs and crawfish. Another to scour Lobsterville Beach for tender baby horseshoe crabs. A third assigned to the beach plumming detail. Afterward we'll share it out family by family. Agreed?" He paused. "As for those garbage boys, we're working on a plan."

"Tell us! Tell us!" everybody shouted.

"I'm afraid that's not possible," said the Oldest Coon. "I'm going to pick a dozen raccoons to help work it out. Even they will be sworn to secrecy."

"Give us a hint," everybody shouted. "Give us a hint!"

The Oldest Coon held up his paw for silence. "I *can* tell you this," he said. "Men pride themselves on being the only creatures with what they call the 'opposable thumb.' That means they can pinch each one of their four claws against the fifth, pick up small objects, and use tools, and build, and tie knots, and cut with terrible knives, and so forth. But I ask you, neighbors, is there another creature you know of with claws and paws that can pinch and sort and do all kinds of smart things like that?"

"Raccoons! Raccoons!" came the reply.

"Right," said the Oldest Coon. "And the skill we use for sorting out garbage or washing our supper, or simply for slithering crawfish out from under rocks, I reckon we can put to a far different task. Now, let's get down to business."

As the assembled raccoons watched, the Oldest Coon had the stage cleared. Then, at his direction two saw-horses were brought up and placed well apart. Next came a long pole. Finally a chair and a small table. On the table he carefully placed a lock, a key, and a big box of Ohio Blue Tip matches.

"All right," the Oldest Coon announced briskly, ignoring the whispering that the sight of these objects stirred in the audience. "All right! First I'm going to call out the names of the dozen raccoons who seem best qualified to make the plan work. I've picked 'em all with a specific job in mind and I hope they turn out to be a daring dozen indeed."

And he began. "Big Benjamin, Fat Frederick, Greasy Gene." There was little surprise at any of these names. To a scattering of applause, the first three left their seats and went to stand beside the Oldest Coon. In addition to being First Selectcoon, Big Benjamin was the biggest and strongest coon on the island. Fat Frederick was the fattest, as well as one of the smartest. Greasy Gene, who lived in a hollow tree near the Allways Garage, went about stained with car oil, but he knew more about men and mechanical things than any other coon on the island.

When the Oldest Coon called out the name "Slick Samuel Coon," though, small, disapproving gasps rose from the crowd. Slick Sam was a weasel-faced coon whom nobody liked — or trusted. It was said of him that he would steal eggs from a baby and many a baby had seen him do it. Besides, Sam lived a very unhealthy sort of life down island, under a shed next to a jewelry store. He wasn't a proper Up Islander at all. Another gasp greeted the name of Clarence Coon, a pale young fellow with rimless glasses who regularly fed upon the leftovers in the garbage can behind the novelty shop where island children bought crayons, notebooks, and costumes for Hallowe'en.

"What can *he* do?" everybody unkindly whispered as Clarence, looking embarrassed and useless as usual, joined the growing group on stage beside the Oldest Coon. These grumblings were silenced, however, by the next choice — Sailor Bill Coon, a popular nautical figure who eked out a living in a sandy spit of land near Thaddeus Hall's Island Boatyard.

The last surprise came when the Oldest Coon stopped calling out names and the audience counted the chosen raccoons. First they counted from left to right. Then they counted from right to left. Then they began to shout.

"The twelfth coon! The twelfth coon! Where's the twelfth coon?"

"All in good time, folks," said the Oldest Coon. "These eleven were picked for qualities that we *know* they have. The twelfth and final member of the daring dozen will have to compete for the job."

3.

Joshua

"The hero we need now," continued the Oldest Coon, "must be one of the quickest and boldest raccoons on the island. But also, one of the *smallest!*" He looked down at the row of kits before him. The young coons, in turn, began to squirm eagerly and look round at their mothers and fathers. "Oh, yes," added the Oldest Coon. "Your parents will have to agree to this dangerous mission."

One by one the little raccoons rushed round to their parents. There were whisperings and exclamations and now and then a voice saying "Please, Mom" or "Gee, Dad, why can't I?" Then, gradually, a half dozen or so small raccoons reported to the stage, ringing themselves around the Oldest Coon.

"Now," he said to them, "you fellows are going to learn what the rope, the pole, and the lock and key and the matches are for. They're to test your skill at certain things you may need to do if you become part of the mission." The parents of the little raccoons exchanged worried glances. The young candidates jostled together nervously.

"The first test," explained the Oldest Coon, "is for balance. As you see, I've put this jiggly, round pole between two sawhorses. You must run across it without falling off before I count five *and* — " He paused for effect. "You will be disqualified if the pole rolls more than an inch to right or left."

One by one the little raccoons clambered up the sawhorse, measured the length of the pole with their eyes, drew a deep breath and scampered across. All except one made it. Anatole Coon, age six, stirred the pole with his left hind paw just as he got across and it rolled an inch or two. He was so sad at having been eliminated that he burst into tears and ran back into the crowd, where he put his head on his relieved mother's lap and refused to look around for a full minute.

Next came the rope trick. The Oldest Coon showed the candidates how to untie a knot, first picking at it with his teeth to loosen it enough so he could get a better grip with his forepaws, then putting his hind foot on one end of the rope for proper purchase while, paw over paw, he hauled on the other end until it had been pulled through the loop.

"You understand," he said, tying another knot in the line, "you must untie this knot before I count to two hundred by fives. Maybe the audience will give me a little help."

So, as the Oldest Coon led off the counting and the crowd chimed in "Five — ten — fifteen — twenty — twenty-five — thirty — thirty-five — forty" one by one, the little coons wrestled with the knot. The first forgot to put his hind paw on the other end of the rope and soon was tangled up like a man trying to unscramble a bowl of spaghetti. "One eighty-five — one ninety — one ninety-five — two hundred!" counted the crowd, its voice rising in excitement as the deadline approached. The small raccoon unwound himself and slunk back into the audience. But the next four young candidates solved the knot problem in time.

"Good work," said the Oldest Raccoon to the remaining four. Turning to the audience he continued. "For the next test I must ask the parents' indulgence. The mission may be dangerous but the test is not. And it is a very good way of measuring just how well a young raccoon can use his paws — and keep calm when he is afraid."

He picked up the big matchbox and turned to the contestants. "I'm going to show you how to take a match out of the box, strike it and then, quickly, put it out. Once it's lit you must dunk it in this little bowl of water — like that." The flaming match made a small hissing noise as it was plunged under water.

Two of the little raccoons had been taught by their parents never to play with matches. They were unable to go through with the test. With shaking paws they did manage to get the box open and take out a match. But when it actually came to striking it along the side of the box their courage failed. Dropping both box and match they too ran down into the crowd. The remaining two candidates had been taught how to use matches under supervision. They blinked and twitched their small whiskers in distaste at the heat and smell of sulphur, but both opened the box, struck flame, and doused it before the crowd could count to fifty by fives.

The last test was the hardest. The Oldest Coon put the key and lock on the floor. The key was to be inserted in the lock, he explained. But not as far as it would go. For the lock would only fly open when the key was turned at a certain depth. That depth each candidate must find — or feel — for himself, by trial and error. The count was to be two hundred and fifty by fives.

The eager crowd began counting aloud again, as the first of the two raccoons left in the contest picked up the key. He had no trouble getting it into the lock. But somehow the exact depth, the exact pressure, the exact twist escaped him. At last, as the sound of the counting crowd rose higher and higher in his ears, he grew desperate. Angrily he banged the lock on the floor to get it open. Stamped on it with his right hind foot. Then threw it down, crashing it on the floor, and ran off the stage. The last little coon fared badly too. When the key would not turn he tried to force it, thrusting it into the lock harder and harder, and twisting it until, if he'd been stronger, the key would have been badly bent. The lock refused to budge. "TWO HUNDRED THIRTY-FIVE — TWO HUNDRED AND FORTY — TWO HUNDRED AND FORTY-FIVE," yelled the crowd. But the whole audience groaned when the count passed two hundred and fifty and all the assembled raccoons realized that the last young candidate had failed.

The Oldest Coon looked a bit puzzled. "Maybe that last test was too hard, folks," he said. "But the mission will take a lot of skill." He looked around the hall. "Would anybody else give it a try?" For a full minute — which is a much longer time than you think until you look at a watch and wait for it to be over — the audience sat in silence. Then a timid voice piped up. "Please, sir. May I try?"

It was Joshua C. Coon. Joshua was nine years old. But he was by far the smallest nine-year-old raccoon on the island. Most of the bigger kits figured he was too small to play acornball and they left him out. If he went to the ball field and waited, hoping to play, nobody ever chose him. Gradually, unlike other children, Joshua got to spending a lot of time fooling around on his own.

He spent hours swinging up and down through the branches of the tree by his nest. He made models out of collections of nuts and shells. He could balance for minutes at a time on a roller skate his father found for him at the dump. Once he even built a boat out of bottle caps and bits of plastic stuck together with abandoned chewing gum. Joshua told himself stories about raccoon heroes but he was so little, and so left out, that he hadn't dared to come forward with the rest.

All the other raccoons whistled, and a few sneered at Joshua's words. But the Oldest Coon smiled kindly at him. "Come right ahead, young fellow." Joshua raced forward. He began the first test almost before the crowd started counting. His feet scarcely touched the pole as he skipped across. He had some trouble with the knot because his right hind leg was so short that he could barely hold down the rope end with it. But just as the count was reaching one hundred and ninety-five Joshua untied it. The match trick was easy, because, I'm sorry to say, Joshua had experimented with matches when his parents were off at the beach. Besides, he had watched the other little raccoons fail. He saw that because they were afraid they held the matches too near the end. When it came time for striking the tip along the rough

edge of the box, they did not have a good grip and could not strike hard enough to make the matches light.

The key and lock were almost Joshua's undoing. As the public counting proceeded he turned and twisted the key. But nothing happened. The count rose steadily. "Seventy-five — eighty — eighty-five — ninety." Finally Joshua closed his eyes, so that only his front paws could feel the key's motion in the lock. Even so, the crowd had barely reached ONE HUNDRED AND FORTY-FIVE when the lock flew open. Joshua leaped in the air from sheer excitement.

"Well done," said the Oldest Coon. "Just join the others over there." Little Joshua sidled over shyly and took his place beside Big Ben. He looked a bit silly standing there beside the enormous raccoon, and some of the crowd, especially the mean young coons who refused to let him play acornball, snickered. But Big Ben put his vast paw out, shook Joshua's hand and growled "Good work, kid."

4.

Some Curious Doings

During the next few days, as the daring dozen worked on the Oldest Coon's mission, they kept very much to themselves. The rest of the Up Island coons knew only that a plan was being perfected. They also noticed that the Oldest Coon was spending a good deal of time each night in the crotch of the cedar tree looking at Ezra Norton's television set. What he was learning there nobody could guess.

For the summer visitors, meanwhile, life went on pretty much as usual. Had they known about the raccoons' food crisis they might have paid more attention than they did to a number of odd and apparently disconnected happenings.

Wednesday morning, for instance, Thad Hall came out of his office at the Island Boatyard and walked over to the wall where most of the sailboat fittings were hung.

"Say, Mary," he asked, turning to the girl who helped out with the stock during the summer season, "don't we have more blocks than this?"

Mary came over and looked. "Well," she said doubtfully, "I sold two last week. But I don't really know. I *did* think there were a few more down there on the lowest row beside the snap shackles." She bent down near the floor where blocks, pulleys, and snap shackles were hanging on a series of S-shaped hooks.

"Only ten left," she said after counting. "I'll have to check the inventory tonight."

"Do that," said Hall, and walked back into his office shaking his head.

On Thursday evening Henry Mayhew, chief mechanic at the New Wampum Chevrolet Service & Garage came home to his wife Madge. He sat looking out over the harbor.

"Anything happen at work today?" Madge asked.

"Only this morning," Henry said. "Fellahs down to the garage don't believe me. Maybe you won't either." There was a longish pause.

"Give me a try," said Madge, after she got tired of waiting.

"Well," said Henry, "you know how I generally go down ahead of the crew to open the place up? Get out the work sheets and so forth?"

Madge nodded.

"Well, this morning," said Henry, "I was in there like always. And I heard a funny noise, you know. A kind of scratching and a squeaking."

"Rats, likely," said Madge.

"Rats, my foot," said Henry Mayhew with some warmth. "It was comin' from Eldridge Edey's 'fifty-eight Chevy pickup. I snuck up to the cab, quiet like, and opened the door real quick. What d'yuh think come out? Why, a big raccoon, that's what come out. Big as you he was, almost. Covered with car grease, too. Been standin' on the seat with his paws up on the steering wheel."

"You're going to sit there and tell me you saw a raccoon at the wheel of El Edey's old truck?" said Madge.

"Not *see* him," protested Henry. "But he was there. Never fear. They was grease marks on the wheel, just like on the seat."

"Mechanics put them there, likely," said Madge. "What do you want for supper?"

The strangest sight of the week was witnessed by Biff Edwards. Biff pumped gas at Allways Garage halfway down island — at least when he was sober enough to do so. When he was drunk he wasn't good for much, though the stories he told after his monthly binges were famous on the island. So famous, and so little believed, that Biff's feelings grew sore. People laughed at his stories so much that he took to keeping his adventures

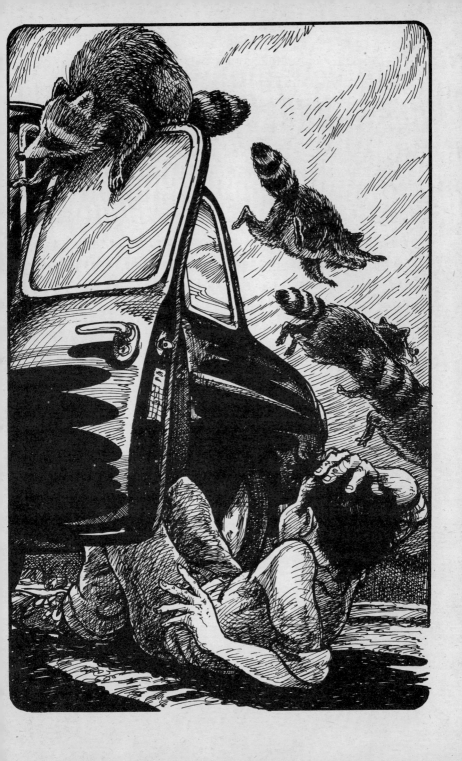

to himself. "You ain't gonna believe me," he would say, stubbornly. "I ain't gonna tell yuh."

Late Friday Biff stopped at Allways, long since closed for the night, to pick up a spare tire he had left there for his old Ford. It was about midnight. After four hours spent in Palmer's Bar & Grill Biff was not at his best. Approaching Allways he stopped with a squawk of the old car's brakes. But he had missed his target by twenty yards. Backing up he bounced the rear bumper off a gas pump, and finally managed to drop anchor with the bow of his balky vessel hard against a picket fence. Getting out, Biff fumbled and grumbled about in the dark until he found the tire. Grunting, he rolled it toward the Ford and after a long struggle, wrestled it into the back seat. "There," said he to it, "now lay still!"

The tire obliged. But just as Biff was opening the car door to climb back in he stopped. There was some kind of confounded commotion going on in an old four-door sedan that, he knew, had been brought in for a change of spark plugs.

"Wat's 'at?" said Biff.

Nobody answered.

Biff weaved toward the sedan and stood swaying before it for a minute. Silence greeted him. Then the noise began again. Reaching forward Biff twisted the front door handle, and wrenching at it, gave it a great pull. When the door swung toward him suddenly he lost his balance, fell backward and found himself sitting on the ground looking into the car. What he thought he saw then he kept to himself, as always. But as Biff drove on home, carefully keeping the white line under the center of his car so the sneaky road wouldn't get away from him, he talked the whole thing over to himself.

"There they was," he mumbled. "All bundled up in there like ticks in a dog's ear. Six of the biggest blamed coons I ever see. They just looked at me awhile. Then they lit out. For a minute there was coons goin' every which way." As a boy Biff had hunted coons with dogs on moonlit nights. He had watched them cleaning out island garbage cans as long as he could remember. But he'd never seen anything like the coon that had been sitting on the front seat of that sedan. "Big," Biff said to himself, as the Ford found its way past Beetlebung Corners. "Big," he said again, still enjoying the memory of it and searching for some way of describing it right. "Big as a dog," he finally muttered to himself. "Broad as a barn door." Nobody would believe him of course. Next day he hardly believed himself.

5.

Alarm Clocks and Excursions

Sunday was a dark night, with a faint drift of fog in the air. Which was good and bad, the Oldest Coon thought. Good, because in the fog everything would look ghostlier and be harder to see. Bad, because — as every islander knows — fog makes sound carry farther. The raccoons had picked the earliest hours of Monday for the daring dozen's mission because, after the weekend, the garbage was always at its richest. Lobster bits in butter. Hearts of celery. Chunks of quiche Lorraine. A coon's ransom in leftover swordfish.

At precisely twelve o'clock midnight Big Benjamin stood in the dark outside the Methodist church. Around him were grouped the rest of the daring dozen, including Joshua, who had been put to bed just before moonrise as usual, and only wakened again a few minutes ago. He was still yawning and rubbing his eyes. Around the daring dozen were thirty or forty more raccoons ranged in squads of four.

"Does everybody have a mask?" Big Ben asked. There were low murmurs of assent. "All right then," Ben went on, "you already have your stations. Wait there till dawn. If nothing happens go home. We'll get word to you somehow if it's on again for tomorrow." The outer ring of coons melted away into the dark. What seemed like total silence fell. Gradually, out of it, the waiting raccoons could make out the bark of a distant dog, and the remote squawk of gulls across the inlet. Joshua Coon edged closer to the others. At last Big Ben spoke again. "All right," he said, "now's our time." And he struck out through the damp fields. Single file, the daring dozen followed.

It was still fully dark when they looked down on the cluster of cottages, the narrow channel running in from the sea, the tangled spars of fishing boats. Below them, in the fog, was the tiny cabin in which Nip Jordan and Tuck Taylor slept. To the left, between the Up Island store and a tiny gray restaurant, the truck *Esmeralda* was parked at the tip of an inlet. As they had been trained to do, eleven raccoons knelt in a circle around Big Ben, who took out a map.

"Here's the route we'll eventually follow," he said. He unfolded another paper. "And here's the plan of the boys' cabin. Nine of you, including Joshua, will come with me. The others will have fifteen minutes' start getting the truck rigged. Greasy Gene?"

"Here."

"You and Bill are in charge of that. If we can spare any we'll get more guys down later to help you."

Five minutes later the two groups separated. Joshua and Big Ben were soon crouched beside the east wall of Nip and Tuck's cabin. To the little raccoon the sheer wooden face of it seemed to climb forever up into the dark sky. He swallowed hard, but said nothing. Ben noticed and patted him on the shoulder.

"You can do it, kid," he rumbled. "Just keep your head, and stick to the old guy's plan. Now everybody, here we go!" On command, Fat Freddy knelt down and leaned against the cabin wall. Big Ben stood on his shoulders. Clarence stood on Big Ben's shoulders. Soon there was a ladder of raccoons straining upward toward the roof. "Quick, Joshua!" grunted Ben. "We can't stay like this forever."

Joshua took another deep breath and began to scramble upward. He was a bit handicapped because he was carrying a folded floor plan of the cabin. Once, on the way up, he put his sharp left hind paw into Clarence Coon's right ear — and heard Clarence stifle a groan. Once he missed his hold on a big coon's head, slipped and almost fell. But at last he reached the top. By standing on his hind legs he could just stretch his forepaws over the edge of the cabin wall where an air space had been left to keep the place cool.

Squirrels and birds often used it in the fall. But the opening was not meant for a raccoon, even the littlest nine-year-old raccoon on the island. Joshua squiggled and squirmed. He tried to go in headfirst. He tried imagining that he was as thin as an eel, but that didn't help either. At last, desperate, he hiked one hind paw up over the edge and scrunched himself in sideways. He found that he was easily able to climb down to a two-by-four plank that ran along near the top of the wall. This was exactly what the plan had told him would happen and he felt much better. He whispered to himself: "Step two successfully completed."

On the two-by-four Joshua paused for a squint at the floor plan. Then he ran along the plank toward the north corner of the room. Halfway there another two-by-four rose at an angle from the floor as a support for the roof frame. Lowering himself onto it, Joshua slithered slowly down. He had come down about five feet, which was supposed to put him exactly over the foot of Tuck Taylor's bed. The Oldest Coon's plan said: "Now jump. Then stay completely still until you have counted to fifty by ones." Joshua jumped and landed on a coverlet with a lump under it. He heard a groan. Like a huge advancing wave the lump rolled toward him.

"What's 'at?" a sleepy voice growled.

Joshua froze. He was so scared that he forgot to count. But he stayed still for a long time.

When all he could hear again was heavy, regular breathing, the little raccoon backed down off the bed, scampered along the floor to a low desk nearby. He bumped into a chair standing beside it. Painfully, he climbed its rungs up to the seat, and then on up its ladder back until he stood teetering on the top. A quick hop brought him to the top of the desk. He paused again for breath. Steps three and four completed. The heart of the mission lay just ahead.

Cautiously he moved forward until his paws identified a large blotter lying on the desk top. Gently he felt his way to one corner of it, and then groped softly under it the way his mother had taught him to feel under rocks for crawfish. Without making any sound except a faint scratching he located, pulled out and put aside: One match. One slip of folded paper. Three cold, thin dimes. One elastic band. Then his paw closed over a key. He was so proud, so relieved — and so eager to escape — that he had already jumped back to the chair top with the key in his teeth before he realized he'd forgotten something. Something terribly important. Something on which the whole mission and — the Oldest Coon had told him — maybe the whole future of Up Island Raccoondom might depend. Back he jumped and began groping around the desk top again. Was it here? Would he find it?

At last his searching paw came in contact with metal

and glass. He felt all over it, like a blind man trying to memorize the face of a new acquaintance. The round curve of metal. The bulging smooth surface of glass. And, yes, the three little knobs, just like the ones Big Ben had made him practice with blindfolded. With all his strength Joshua pushed one of the knobs in.

A huge sigh of relief escaped him. He felt suddenly light, as if he could fly. Or at least leap from the desk to the roof beam in a single bound. He spun round to jump for the chair. His tail swung carelessly after him in the dark, hitting Tuck Taylor's alarm clock which slid toward the desk edge, tilted there for an instant in the dark, then clanged to the floor. Joshua tried to turn himself into stone. It seemed to him that the roof would fall in. That the crash could be heard from there to Edgartown. Maybe even as far as Boston.

If the alarm clock bell went off, or the cabin lights went on, Big Ben had told him, he was to run under the bed and wait. Neither of these things happened. All he heard was the same deep, sleepy voice calling, "Who's there?" After a second a large human paw began reaching slowly out across the desk, just missing Joshua. Then the little raccoon could hear it groping around somewhere below him in the darkness. "Oh, no!" the sleepy voice grumbled, "Blasted clock fell off again." The blasted clock then appeared over the side of the desk and was set down next to Joshua. Bedsprings creaked

as Tuck Taylor settled himself for sleep again. Across the cabin another voice growled. "Tuck, knock off that racket. We've got a run to make at five this morning." Then silence. As he waited, without moving a whisker, Joshua began to count his heartbeats. When he got to fifty he thought it would be all right to put his paws on the alarm clock again — to see if the little knob was still safely pushed in. It was.

Joshua hopped to the chair top. Scrambled down the ladder rungs. Clawed his way up the bedspread. Leapt from the bed to the slanting two-by-four. Pattered upward until he could hoist himself onto the ridge of the wall. Peeking out he chittered very softly. After a moment he could hear the other raccoons grunting as they formed their pyramid again. He swung himself down into the darkness, hanging by his front paws this time, and let go his hold half afraid that he would drop straight down and smash on the dirt around the cabin. But his hind paws felt the warm, furry shoulder of Clarence Coon. In a few seconds he was on the ground, the other raccoons clustered around him.

"I got the blasted clock," Joshua yelped, gasping for breath. "And here's the key you wanted."

"You did good, kid," said Big Ben. Then they all ran for the truck.

6.

Esmeralda, Farewell

The sun was high in the sky and the gulls on Gull Island had already been trying to deafen the world for hours when Nip Jordan opened his eyes. He lay for a minute or two. Then, noticing how bright the day was outside, he jumped out of bed. "Tuck, Tuck!" he yelled and, striding across the cabin, began to shake his partner awake.

"Wha, what?" mumbled Tuck Taylor.

"We're late," screamed Nip. "Blasted alarm didn't go off."

Tuck stuck bare feet into dirty sneakers and began throwing on work clothes. "It's after ten o'clock. We should have finished the run by now."

"I'll start up *Esmeralda*," said Nip, heading for the door still buttoning his shirt.

"Coming, boss," Tuck called after him. He shuffled out the cabin door still trying to get his right foot fully into a torn sneaker, and stumbled straight into Nip Jordan's back.

"Cool it, buddy," said Nip. "Cool it."

"Whuddya mean, cool it?"

"I mean *cool* it." He nodded glumly down the hill. "Some chump has ripped off *Esmeralda*."

Tuck considered the empty spot where the garbage truck always stood. "What has four wheels and flies?" he asked.

"Fun-nee," said Nip. "What'll we do now?"

"Call the fuzz," said Tuck. "Unless you buy my flying theory. There's a phone at the store."

"You gotta be kidding," said Nip. "We phone from *there* everybody on this island'll know what's happened. *And* begin yowling about what's going to happen to their garbage. Let's try Mrs. Tilton's."

Mrs. Tilton was the last stop on their garbage run — at the foot of Flounders Lane. She was also the boys' favorite client. After they had stopped by about nine in the morning on their first run she was so pleased with their work that she thanked them personally. Since then she and Pamela, her young golden retriever, had often greeted the boys — Pamela by prancing around and asking to play ball, Mrs. Tilton with plates of blueberry pie and cups of coffee.

"Come in, boys," she said as she saw them approaching her back porch. "You sure were early this morning."

"We're sorry about the garbage, Mrs. Tilton," Nip said. "We overslept."

"Overslept?" Mrs. Tilton was obviously puzzled. "When you came by this morning it was still dark. I figured you'd just switched me round on your route."

"When we came by?" asked Tuck.

"Why, yes," Mrs. Tilton twinkled at them. "Oh, I know you try to be quiet. And you *are* quiet. Quietest garbage crew we've ever had. But I couldn't sleep last night. 'Bout three in the morning I was lying there awake. That's how I came to hear your truck — and the shifting of the cans." She smiled. "Funny thing, though. Pam barked at you. Didn't you hear her? Deep in her throat the way she does when she's real mad."

Tuck was already edging toward the door. "Uh, thanks, Mrs. Tilton," he said. "We gotta be going. Come on, Nip."

The two boys walked up the dusty road in silence.

Finally Tuck said, "What kind of a creep would wait till the middle of the night, steal a garbage truck *and* collect the garbage?"

"Maybe they just did Mrs. Tilton to make the joke look good," said Nip. "We'll probably find the cans bulging on the rest of the run." But along Flounders Lane all the houses had empty cans. What's more, there wasn't a scrap of trash anywhere. That day not a single complaining phone call about uncollected garbage came for Nip and Tuck at the Up Island store.

Nip got more impatient as the day wore on.

"Joke or not," he fumed, "I'm going to call the police."

"You sound like some off-islander," said Tuck with a grin. "Like there was some kind of SWAT team here with radar and bullhorns, the whole bit. When you say police here, buddy, you mean Chief Harley Stark."

"So?" Nip growled.

"Harley Stark couldn't find a bear in a telephone booth."

"He could find our truck," Nip replied. "That'd do for starters."

"You and I can find the truck," said Tuck. "After jockeying *Esmeralda* into every sand pit at this end of the island we know the places better than anybody."

"And when we find her what'll we do?" asked Nip.

"We'll watch her," said Tuck.

"Watch her!" exploded Nip. "And let those creeps, whoever they are, get away with murder?"

"You've missed the whole point," said Tuck with a grin. " 'Those creeps, whoever they are,' have just done a day's work for us. I want to know why."

It took Nip and Tuck till Wednesday afternoon — afoot and on borrowed bikes — to find *Esmeralda*. She was parked deep in the scrub oak at the end of a bumpy trail way out beyond the town dump. Unharmed. Totally clean. Empty of garbage. Without a key. Even her admiring swarm of flies had abandoned her.

"Well?" said Nip.

"I'm glad you asked that question," said Tuck. "Tomorrow's garbage day. Starting at midnight we'll set up a watch."

"And if nobody comes?"

"If nobody comes by five," said Tuck, "we'll use my spare key — " he hauled it out of his jeans to wave at Nip — "and go into our regular old Nip Jordan–Tuck Taylor garbage disappearance act again."

Just after midnight Nip and Tuck were crouched in the weeds behind a tree thinking deeply about ticks and poison ivy. Their bikes were parked up a little lane not far away. In front of them on the back porch of Harrison Frazier's house, one of the earlier stops on their normal route, stood three bulging trash cans. Nip was having trouble staying awake, partly because he figured this was going to be a wasted trip. Sometimes his head would drop down on his chest. When he started to snore Tuck usually nudged him. But as the hours passed Tuck gave it up. Nip was soon full asleep. He dreamed that a giant alligator had taken over the garbage run, clanking along from house to house, flipping the full cans into the air and swallowing their contents.

The alligator was huge and green and Nip was just

noticing that it had eyes like *Esmeralda*'s headlights when he heard a voice. "Nip! Nip!" it called. He groggily shook his head. Tuck seemed to be shaking him. Then Tuck hissed. "Great holy pastrami, look at that!"

The Fraziers kept a small, yellow, antibug light burning on their back porch. In its dim rays, as if still in a dream, Nip glimpsed a curious spectacle. A dozen raccoons were moving about on the porch. Acting like a team of well-trained acrobats, they hoisted a garbage can on their shoulders and moved off with it. In the faint light it looked as if the can had just acquired a lot of silent, furry wheels and rolled away.

Down the steps it went and along the path to the road, the boys stealthily watching. There stood *Esmeralda,* her motor chugging over gently. Another squad of coons came to meet the can carriers. There was a good deal of chittering and growling. The coons seemed to be attaching some lines to the can's handles. Then the two squads of coons separated, each pulling on a line that ran to a block and tackle on the truck frame. The can swayed slowly upward. When it hung opposite the mouth of the truck's huge garbage bin, two coons scrambled up beside it, grabbed one end and tipped the contents of the can into the bin's dark maw. One waved his arm. The hauling squads let out line, lowering the can to the ground. Then more raccoons carried it back down the path to the house.

"Do you see what I see?" whispered Nip. Tuck jabbed him to be quiet.

The remaining raccoons went forward toward the cab of the truck. The boys could just make out their plump forms, as they clambered up onto the steel running board. The truck cab doors opened, then closed. Nip started to move from the hiding place so he could get a better look but Tuck held him tight to the ground.

"Mustn't scare 'em," he muttered.

As the two boys watched, *Esmeralda* slowly began to move forward and turn. The truck moved awkwardly. Then stopped. A curious clanking and the sound of a good deal of chittering came from the cab. But gradually *Esmeralda* backed up, made her turn and began to lumber down the road into the darkness, on her way, no doubt, to the Weesmer place.

"My summer job," chortled Tuck. "Hijacked by raccoons!" He jumped up and wheeled his bicycle out of the weeds.

Nip was still confused. "How d'yuh suppose the little critters do it?" he asked.

"No time to talk," Tuck called back over his shoulder. He was already walking his bike swiftly up the sandy road. "Got to get to the dump ahead of them." He swung himself into the seat. Nip stood looking after him for a moment, then, still shaking his head in wonder, followed.

7.

On the Road

Inside the cab of *Esmeralda* as she jostled from stop to stop along the garbage route, things were as busy and crowded as a sailboat cockpit during a race. The raccoons had had some considerable practice in handling the truck by then, but it was still a problem. On the right side of the cab sat little Joshua with a clipboard and a list of the regular stops, both of them part of *Esmeralda*'s regular equipment. The rest of the cab was pretty well filled up with raccoons and the nautical hardware they had rigged to help them manage the truck.

At the wheel, his head and forepaws visible through the window from outside, was Big Ben wearing an old-fashioned boater hat as a disguise. He was able to reach and grip the wheel properly because he was standing on Fat Freddy who, with his tail curled around his nose, had obligingly turned himself into a large, round, self-propelled cushion.

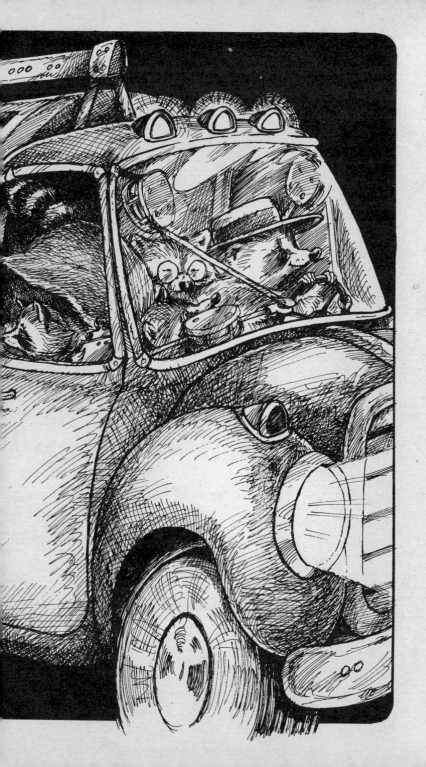

Ben could handle the automatic gearshift lever with his strong right forepaw. When he needed to turn *Esmeralda,* he twisted the wheel with all his might, at the same time shouting "port" or "starboard" depending on whether the turn was to left or right. From the floor of the cab on either side a three-coon hauling squad would then lay back on lines that Sailor Bill had rigged through two blocks, one fixed on one side of the wheel, one fixed on the other, and both anchored on pulleys secured to the truck's upper door hinges.

Greasy Gene and Sailor Bill acted as a roving floor team. If Ben chittered a command to put down the lights, one of them would scramble over and punch the floor button that lowered *Esmeralda*'s high beams. If braking was called for, the two would lean on the foot brake with all their strength. Otherwise Gene sat curled against the gas pedal exerting just enough pressure to keep *Esmeralda* moving at a safe clip. When it came time to start the motor Joshua became the key figure. Dropping the clipboard he would run forward across the seat, then, scrambling over to Greasy Gene's shoulders, try to turn the ignition key — while Sailor Bill took over the gas pedal. The first time Joshua attempted this he teetered a bit, then dropped the key. But under Ben's unflappable direction, and with plenty of practice, Joshua had grown quite expert.

Fortunately for the hijackers, *Esmeralda*'s route lay

mainly along back roads. And the late hour of the night, or the earliness of morning, meant there were few cars either to be passed, or seen by. Once they had a close call. Running down island along a short stretch of state road, they met a station wagon with its headlights up, coming toward them. Big Ben, who had stowed away in the back seat of an Island-Drive-Yourself Driver's School sedan for instruction before the mission, did his best to remember what he had heard. Turning his eyes toward the edge of the road ahead — to keep from being temporarily blinded — he chittered a command to Greasy Gene to ease off a bit on the gas pedal. *Esmeralda* slowed. There was consternation in the cab when the other car slowed down — noticeably — though only Ben could actually see it. For a second or two the driver peered curiously into *Esmeralda,* then speeded up again.

The raccoons breathed a sigh of relief when at last they were able to turn off the state road into Quincy Lane for a pickup at the house of G. R. Strangeways. But they would have worried less had they heard the conversation just then taking place in the station wagon.

"Whew, Maude!" said the driver. "For a second there I'd have sworn the man at the wheel was a big raccoon with a hat and mask."

"Now, John," said his wife soothingly. "I told you to go easy on the brandy after dinner. That was just those two kids, likely, using their garbage truck for a fancy dress party. Anyway," she added, "raccoons all wear masks, don't they?"

As *Esmeralda*, fully loaded, was groaning over the final few hundred yards to the dump Sailor Bill looked up from the floor of the cab and glimpsed the moon through the window.

"Great work, mates," Bill sang out. "We're finishing earlier tonight than last Monday." The daring dozen cheered. But the old truck lost several minutes trying to navigate the final hairpin turn into the dump area. The raccoons had to back her up several times. Greasy Gene stalled *Esmeralda* once, too, when he failed to lean his haunch hard enough on the gas pedal as they started. But Joshua skinned up onto Gene's shoulders in short order, turned the key, and they were off again.

When *Esmeralda* had finally stopped beside the littered expanse of the dump, pale in the moonlight, with gauzy scarfs of white mist streaming over it, the daring dozen tumbled out. The Oldest Coon, who had been waiting, walked out to a small hill of refuse and looked around carefully. He considered the dark woods, the piles of crates, the rolling heaps of ashes. He looked and listened with care, but neither saw nor heard Nip Jordan and Tuck Taylor who were still and motionless — though highly uncomfortable — crouched in the crotch of a scrub oak that overlooked the scene.

At last the Oldest Coon lifted a silver bo'sun's pipe to his lips and, like one of Robin Hood's men, blew one shrill blast. In an instant the boys were looking down on a scene that no human eye had ever witnessed before. Out of the dark woods small, furry shapes began to pour into the dump area from every direction. Squads, platoons, companies, regiments of raccoons they were, and they massed themselves around the Oldest Coon. At his command, they set to work.

The last garbage was hauled down out of *Esmeralda* and placed beside earlier loads. Then the first rough sorters swarmed over the pile, separating food from trash. All edibles in one pile. In another all milk cartons, plastic spoons, crinkled tinfoil, clusters of cans, stained sponges, defunct mops, splintered broom handles, wadded Kleenex, cardboard toilet paper cores, murderous chunks of broken glass, dog-munched Frisbees, tired toothbrushes, whole families of empty wine bottles, baseball cards drowned in orange juice or Hawaiian Punch, balsa-wood gliders with smashed wings, the occasional old sock, its years of monogamy over (raccoon mothers saved the woolen ones for winter quilting), stack on stack of bottle caps, now and then a silver fork, sheer towers of frozen food packages. Everything was gone over, emptied of anything to drink, scraped clean of anything to eat, then carted off and placed in a separate pile in the middle of the dump. The piles were

then set alight by a small team of specially trained coons, ceremonially led by young Joshua.

As the flames danced high and the smoke from burning plastic swirled in black eddies behind them, raccoon legions set upon the assembled mountains of food. Once again — as Nip Jordan and Tuck Taylor soon saw — to separate the good from the bad.

A special squad seemed to be setting standards. The reeking bits of meat and fruit that did not pass muster, the far-gone pork chops and antique bacon rinds were all placed on small plastic trays — the kind used in supermarkets for meat displays — and carried toward the consuming flames, like ancient heroes bound for burial, upon the shoulders of six stalwart raccoons.

All the good food — there were still piles and piles of it — was gradually pushed or patted onto similar trays and hoisted onto shoulders by local forage parties for carrying to dens and hollow trees. The last item that the watching boys noticed was a large, almost perfect watermelon that had gone astray at a picnic. It was borne away by eight raccoons — a row of four to each side — like a big, dark green spaceship in a science-fiction film being lugged off by a crew of hairy giants.

8.

Feast or Famine

The following night in the basement of the Methodist church, the Benevolent Protective Society of Raccoons held a harvest home dinner. Rich dishes garnered from the dump alternated with courses contributed by raccoon teams assigned to forage in tidal creeks and salt marshes, not to mention several forays into Farmer Greene's expensive cornfields. The cranberry juice flowed like water. So did gin and rum and whiskey, which some of the more pleasure-loving raccoons had collected by drips and drops from bottles at the dump. To the great joy of the raccoon kits, especially Joshua, Captain Crunch was offered for dessert, along with sugared newts, an old island confection.

I am sorry to say that a number of raccoons got very drunk, which is the worst sort of manners in any animal. They banged on the tables with fists and spoons and again and again howled verses of the same old songs in which words like *June* and *Tune, Moon* and *Coon* were frequently rhymed. A special, ear-splitting favorite was "Raccoon Ramble." Some raccoons even grew sick and had to be removed from the table for their own — and everybody else's — good! They behaved, in fact, a good deal like some men and women.

The noise of chittering and chatting and chanting grew louder and louder. Obstreperous young teen-age coons at one corner of the table kept yelling "DARING DOZEN! DARING DOZEN! DARING DOZEN!" over and over again. At last the Oldest Coon rose to his feet. "Friends," he said. "Friends." The room grew quiet, mainly because it was clear he would propose some toasts that all the raccoons had been waiting for.

"At this time of thanksgiving it is a great pleasure to be able to raise not just one glass but twelve glasses in a row."

Cries of "Hear! Hear!" from the old, "Right on" from the young.

One by one the Oldest Raccoon paid tribute to the daring dozen: Big Ben for being captain of the group, and Slick Sam for stealing all the equipment, and Clarence for providing masks and disguises. When he got to Sailor Bill he cried, "I give you Sailor Bill! It was his blocks that let us tackle the job." The room drank and roared. "Next," continued the Oldest Coon, "I raise my glass to a comrade who served as the very foundation of our enterprise. There is a great deal to him, so much in fact, that to do him justice would take longer than I dare. I give you none other than Fat Frederick."

Cries of delight greeted these remarks. Everybody drank deep, and Frederick bobbed his head and twitched his whiskers in acknowledgment.

"Last," the Oldest Coon said, as the crowd began to cheer. "Last, friends, I want to do honor to as fine a comrade as ever performed perilous scout work in an enemy camp. In years to come it will be said of him that when the alarm clock struck the ground, he knew there wasn't a second to spare. I give you Joshua, the smallest *and* the bravest of our crew."

The assembled raccoons raised their glasses. They drank and shouted and shouted and drank while the little raccoon turned red to the ears and stared miserably into his glass of cranberry juice, almost wishing that his mother had refused to let him stay up for the dinner after all.

Things quieted down. Soon, however, groups of teen-age coons were heard from again. Some kept yelling "Oldest Coon! Oldest Coon! Oldest Coon!" Others chanted "Man with a plan! Man with a plan!" Finally Big Ben rose, quieted them and turned to the Oldest Coon.

"You gave us the plan. But we're going to ask you for

one thing more. A speech." His words were drowned out by shouts of "Speech! Speech! Speech!" The teenage coons were singing "Stand up! Stand up! We won't shut up until you stand up!"

The Oldest Coon rose and waved his paw. "I usually talk too much," he began. "And I fear tonight will be no exception. I can give you some good news. (*Cheers!*) But I have to give you some bad news too. (*Groans.*) First the good news! (*Cheers again.*) We're all together and we've eaten well. (*Cheers!*) And drunk well too! (*Wild cheers!*) And it looks as if we'll eat well for a while now. And yes, I'm pleased to admit it, partly thanks to the plan. (*Cheers!*) But more thanks, a lot more if you ask me, to the raccoons who had the will and the skill to carry it out! (*Shouts of 'For he's a jolly good fellow!'*)

"Now I have a confession to make. As you know, during these last weeks I've spent a good deal of time up in the cedar tree, watching that television machine on Norton's porch. As some of you also know, times past I've figured what you see there is pretty near worthless. Men shooting at other men and running away and everybody jumping into automobiles and tearing around and then shooting some more. Only shooting I ever saw in my own life was one cold, moonlit night in November, when Farmer Greene blew my grandfather, Isaac Coon, out of a hemlock tree. But every raccoon knows that where guns are concerned, the less seen of 'em the better."

The Oldest Coon paused to look into his glass, then drained the few drops remaining in it.

"That television machine can give you silly ideas. Sitting in the crotch of that cedar, trying to figure out what we ought to do, there were moments when I went half crazy. I thought maybe we should steal a wooden gun from some store here on the island, and jump on the running board of that truck, and keep those boys prisoner until we got more garbage. Men call that kidnapping," added the Oldest Coon. "Though I reckon raccoons would have to call it *kitnapping.* (*Long groan from the audience.*)

"Anyway, neighbors, I've got to give credit where credit is due. I finally did get the idea for the plan by watching pictures of some men who planned and carried out a whole 'operation,' or 'mission,' I've forgotten what they called it. But it's always supposed to be impossible and then they do it. And so did we. (*Long cheers.*)

"Now for the bad news. (*Groans again.*) I got that on the television machine too. A gray-haired man sits there and talks and talks — pretty much the way I do. (*Laughter.*) Then, just when you can hardly stand it anymore (*more laughter*) they have some pictures. Don't amount to much, most of 'em. But still, it was on

61

the *news* that I learned something important. It is this. Men are beginning to worry about garbage. They're trying to get rid of it in new ways — and not by leaving it in dumps or giving it to hungry raccoons either, I'm sorry to say. (*Laughter.*) One way the gray-haired man told about, was to take it all, big piles of it, and crunch it down and square it off about the size and shape of one of the big cartons we see stacked behind the Up Island store. And then burn it, to help keep their houses warm in winter."

Astonished cries of "That don't make sense" and "Can't be!"

"Don't anybody doubt it," declared the Oldest Coon, raising his voice. "On that machine I saw pictures of men actually doing it. And that means our rich old garbage days are numbered. Not right off, of course. For this summer we'll just have to see what those boys decide to do about our plan. Even next summer things may be all right, providing they get a sloppy crew to replace these two. But there'll come a time when the garbage'll run out. And we've got to prepare. And that means any young scalawag here who thinks no newts is good newts may get to be a pretty skinny raccoon unless he learns to think differently."

9.

Happy Ending

While the full but now slightly fearful raccoons were trying to digest their dinner — and the Oldest Coon's scary message — Nip Jordan and Tuck Taylor were halfway across the island, on South Beach, enjoying the moonlight on the water. Tuck, anyway, was comfortably stretched out on the sand. Nip was pacing nervously up and down and making plans that would have chilled the hearts of the raccoons if they had heard him.

"Sit down, buddy," said Tuck. "You're spoiling the view."

"Nuts to the view," said Nip. "We're onto something that's going to make scientific history and you just lie there."

"I can see the headlines now," said Tuck, and he held up an imaginary newspaper in the dim light. "UP ISLANDERS OUTWITTED BY RACCOONS."

Nip kept pacing and muttering to himself. "Gotta move fast. Get an infrared camera up here. Get pictures. Otherwise nobody'll ever believe us. Maybe get some raccoon experts up here, too, in case anybody says we faked the photos. And maybe write about it for a magazine."

"Rave on," said Tuck.

"Listen," said Nip. "You wouldn't know a breakthrough in animal behavior if it bit you in the tail. But take it from me, everybody has been going ape for years now about what men can learn from beasts. When I prove that a pack of raccoons can hijack a truck, baby, I'll be famous."

"So will the coons," said Tuck mildly.

"So what?" asked Nip.

"So everything," said Tuck. "Don't you understand anything? Listen! You start rushing around, taking infrared pictures of our furry friends, writing them up for *Scientific American*, trotting in professors, what's gonna happen? First thing you know those coons'll be penned up somewhere for observation, or busy posing for photographers. What they *won't* be doing is collecting garbage."

"Well?" said Nip.

"What's the date?" asked Tuck.

"July sixth."

"And our job runs through Labor Day?"

"Yeah," said Nip. "So?"

"So this," said Tuck. "Those little geniuses are going to provide us with a two-, count 'em, two-month paid vacation on one of the niftiest islands in the world. Next year, too. All we have to do is collect the fees. And keep our mouths shut. Okay?"

For a while the other stood silent looking down at the sand.

"Okay," said Nip Jordan finally. And he grinned.